*For my friend Mapy Seidel who
shows me beautiful things.* — B.M.J.

*For Josephine of El Rosario
for her yellow lollypops.
And for Kieran.* — G.P.

Text copyright © 2001 by Barbara M. Joosse.
Illustrations copyright © 2001 by Giselle Potter.
Discussion guide written by Nicholas Glass © 2001 by Chronicle Books.

Book design by Kristine Brogno.
Typeset in Goudy and Historical Fell Type.
The illustrations in this book were rendered in ink, watercolors and colored pencils.
Printed in Hong Kong.
ISBN 0-8118-2164-1

Library of Congress Cataloging-in-Publication Data
Joosse, Barbara M.
Ghost Wings / by Barbara M. Joosse ; illustrated by Giselle Potter.
p. cm.
Summary: While celebrating the Days of the Dead, a young Mexican girl remembers
her wonderful grandmother who sang songs, made tortillas,
chased away monsters, and loved butterflies.
ISBN 0-8118-2164-1
[1. Grandmothers—Fiction. 2. Death—Fiction. 3. All Souls' Day—Fiction.
4. Butterflies—Fiction. 5. Mexico—Fiction.] I. Potter, Giselle, ill. II. Title.
PZ7.J7435 Gj 2001
[E]–dc21   00-011183

Distributed in Canada by Raincoast Books
9050 Shaughnessy Street
Vancouver, British Columbia V6P 6E5

10 9 8 7 6 5 4 3 2

Chronicle Books LLC
85 Second Street, San Francisco, California 94105

www.chroniclekids.com

Ghost
Wings

by **Barbara M. Joosse** ✳ illustrated by **Giselle Potter**

chronicle books · san francisco

There's a place in the Mexican forest where monarch butterflies go. In the autumn, millions arrive to rest in oyamel fir trees, sip from nectaring plants and fan their wings in the sun. In the spring, they begin their journey north. This place is called the Magic Circle.

I remember the day the butterflies left.

They were the color of the sun setting on the mountains. They filled the trees with gold, so many they made the boughs bend. When they flew away their wings rustled like skirts. That was the day my grandmother died.

Grandmother was my best friend.

When we made tortillas, we sang our favorite songs. Grandmother worked the dough on a big metate, pushing and mashing 'til it didn't have any lumps. I had a little metate, right next to hers. When the tortillas were ready, we cooked them side by side.

At night, Mama tucked me into bed. But I heard monsters slither on the floor. They snapped their teeth and hissed my name. I pulled the covers up to my chin, but still the monsters slithered and snapped.

I cried out to Papa. He said, "You must be brave."

I called to Mama. She said, "Nonsense. There are no monsters."

But Grandmother leaned her broom against my bed and laid beside me, smelling of cornmeal and roses. "If the monsters dare to come," she said, "I'll chase them away with my broom."

With Grandmother next to me, no monsters snapped their teeth, and none of them hissed my name.

In *winter,* Grandmother and I loved to visit the Magic Circle. We sat on the forest floor and let the butterflies cover us with gold. We let them fan their wings on our shoulders and tickle our arms with their legs.

One *spring,* Grandmother became thin as smoke. She didn't make tortillas; she was too tired. She said, "It's almost time for the butterflies to leave. Come with me to the Magic Circle, and we'll say goodbye."

It was a cloudy day, and the butterflies clung to the trees. Their wings were closed, and they were still as stone. One butterfly lay on the forest floor. I picked him up and blew warm breath on him. He shook his wings and flew away.

EXTENSION

"Close your eyes," Grandmother said. "Do you still feel the butterfly?" I nodded. My arm still tickled.

"That's because they carry the souls of the old ones, and the old ones never really leave."

Then the sun came out. The butterflies rose in a whoosh. They filled the sky with gold.

In a few weeks all the butterflies were gone. The Magic
Circle was empty. That was the day Grandmother died.

Papa took me to the Magic Circle and we cried together.
He said when you love someone, they never really leave.
But the butterflies were gone. He said the butterflies would
come back, that they always came back. But my arm didn't
feel the tickle any more.

That night, the monsters crouched beneath my bed and hissed my name. I trembled in my bed alone. I wanted Grandmother! I leaned her broom against my bed and pressed my nose into her pillow. At first I could smell cornmeal and roses, but after a while even the smell was gone.

There was no one between me and the monsters.

The time of the roses passed and became the time of the marigolds.

This was the season for Days of the Dead, the time to remember the old ones. At the market, we bought candles and pan de los muertos with sugar bones on top. Mama chose a bag of oranges, and when I smelled them they made my nose prickle. I bought a little skull made of chocolate and sugar.

After lunch, Papa set up an ofrenda. On it, Mama put candles, oranges and Grandmother's picture. I leaned her broom against the altar, and spread rose petals and cornmeal on top. When the day was almost gone, the light became thin as smoke. Mama lit the candles, and their flames shook the shadows from the room.

Papa said, "I remember Grandmother."

Mama said, "I remember that she taught me how to cook."

I tried to remember Grandmother, too, but she seemed far away. All night, the candles flickered on the ofrenda. I smelled roses and cornmeal as I went to sleep.

In the morning, we walked to the cemetery. All the neighbors were there. We cleaned up the graves of the old ones. I spread flowers over Grandmother's grave and ate my chocolate and sugar skull.

The neighbors filled the cemetery with picnic baskets and flowers, stories and noise. One man sang Grandmother's favorite songs.

There was a tiny flicker in the sky. It was a butterfly.

Soon the tombs and crosses were covered with flickering gold. One of the butterflies landed on my arm. It fanned the sun with its wings and tickled my arm with its legs.

I said, "I remember that Grandmother was brave. She chased monsters with her broom. I remember how she smelled, like cornmeal and roses. She sang songs and made tortillas and when she took me to the Magic Circle it really was full of magic."

The butterfly shook its wings and flew away.

I closed my eyes. I could still feel the tickle. In my head, I heard Grandmother's songs. I smelled roses and cornmeal.

Now, I remembered Grandmother.

Days of the Dead ✳ Los Dias de los Muertos

In the United States, death is often a taboo subject, but not in Mexico. There, Days of the Dead are celebrated between October 31 and November 2. It's a joyful time when the living celebrate the lives of those who have died. By being remembered, the spirits of the dead remain a part of the living.

Many traditions are connected to this fiesta, all of which help to create a lively atmosphere.

Calacas, handmade Days of the Dead skeleton figurines, are placed on the ofrendas or las tumbas. Calacas often represent a favorite activity of a relative such as dancing or playing a guitar.

Calaveras, chocolate and sugar skulls, are given to the children as a treat.

Ofrendas, altars, are set up as offerings to help remember people who have died. Family members put candles, pan de los muertos, photographs, food and familiar objects on top of the altar. Relatives talk about the ones who have died, telling stories and asking for their help with "earthly" problems.

Pan de los muertos, "bread of the dead," is bought at the market. Each anise-flavored loaf is decorated with sugar "bones" or angel faces.

Las tumbas, the graves, are where relatives gather to celebrate. The graves are cleaned and weeded and then the old ones' favorite foods are set out — it is said the dead inhale the "essence" of the food, leaving the rest for the living to eat — along with armloads of flowers and calacas.

Monarch Butterflies

Monarch butterflies winter in the mountains of Mexico. They roost in the oyamel fir forests, gaining strength for their migration north. There are thirteen different preserves in Mexico, home to three hundred million butterflies.

The annual migration begins at Easter, when the first butterflies leave Mexico. They ride the winds to Texas, where they lay eggs on the underside of milkweed leaves. Each parent butterfly dies, leaving up to four hundred eggs to hatch a few days later. Within two weeks the caterpillar — now three thousand times its birth weight — spins a chrysalis and becomes a butterfly.

This butterfly moves further north and begins the eggs-caterpillar-butterfly cycle again. This cycle occurs five times, with each new generation flying further north until the fifth generation reaches the northern United States and Canada. Finally, the fifth generation leaves its northern home and flies up to two thousand miles to return to Mexico.

How do butterflies born in the Unites States find their way back to Mexico, a place they have never been? How does such a delicate insect fly so far? How is it that they arrive in exactly the right place, at the same time every year? Scientists are studying these mysteries by "tagging" butterflies with tiny gummed stickers to track their progress.

Each year, the monarch butterflies return to Mexico during the Days of the Dead. Many people believe they carry the souls of the old ones — the relatives who have died.

A Guide to Using This Book

Ghost Wings captures the special relationship between a girl and her grandmother, who is also her best friend. It reveals the spirit of a place they shared, the Magic Circle, and shows how butterflies are much more than just beautiful creatures. *Ghost Wings* offers opportunities for discussion about feelings, remembrance and relationships. As the book is read aloud, allow time for children to look closely at the illustrations and to ask questions. Reread specific passages that might help children focus on the discussion questions and activities included in this guide.

Feelings

Questions

• The girl loves her grandmother. Can you find a picture that shows this?

• Besides love, what other feelings does the little girl have for her grandmother? Can you find a picture showing these feelings?

Activities

• The girl and her grandmother like to do many things together. List the different activities they share.

• Think of someone you love. What do you like to do with him or her? Write a story or draw a picture of this.

• One way that the illustrator, Giselle Potter, demonstrates the girl's love for her grandmother is by showing the two of them looking at or touching each other. Think of two people you know who love each other and draw a picture of them together.

• The girl loves to visit the Magic Circle with Grandmother. Is there a special place you share with someone you love? Draw a picture or write a story about that place.

Memories

Questions

• Grandmother's family put special things on her ofrenda. What do you see on Grandmother's ofrenda? What other things would you put on the table to remember Grandmother?

• Days of the Dead are a time when people in Mexico remember the lives of loved ones who have died. How do the people in *Ghost Wings* celebrate Days of the Dead?